Scientific and archeological evidence has revealed that some societal advancements made thousands of years ago rival or exceed discoveries made during our Age of Technology!

Proof of this can be found in the stunning achievements of ancient Egyptian architecture, communication and art. From the confounding perfection of the pyramids to the use of pictures as communication devices, ancient Egyptian creations have captivated the brightest of minds.

Recently the universal hunger for ancient Egyptian texts, artifacts and pictographs has uncovered an even more provocative discovery: that at the base of the ancient Egyptians' complex, advanced civilization lay a sophisticated religion that is now commonly called Egyptian Magick.

Find out how this complex religious/magical system inspired the Egyptians' unparalleled productions and what elements of this unmatched culture influence our world today in *The Truth About Egyptian Magick*. As you explore the fascinating culture of the ancient Egyptians, you'll soon understand why theirs is the cornerstone of all modern religion, occultism and magick!

About the Authors

Gerald J. Schueler, born in Darby, Pennsylvania, and his wife Betty Sherlin Schueler, born in Washington D.C., currently reside in Maryland. Jerry is a systems analyst, freelance writer, editor and artist. Betty is a computer consultant, freelance writer, editor, and artist. The Schuelers have co-authored many articles on anthropology, computers, children, dogs, philosophy, magick, and other subjects.

To Write to the Authors

If you wish to contact the authors or would like more information about this book, please write to the authors in care of Llewellyn Worldwide and we will forward your request. Both the authors and publisher appreciate hearing from you and learning of your enjoyment of this book and how it has helped you. Llewellyn Worldwide cannot guarantee that every letter written to the authors can be answered, but all will be forwarded. Please write to:

Gerald and Betty Schueler
c/o Llewellyn Worldwide
P.O. Box 64383-735, St. Paul, MN 55164-0383, U.S.A.

Please enclose a self-addressed, stamped envelope for reply,
or $1.00 to cover costs.
If outside U.S.A., enclose International postal reply coupon.

Free Catalog From Llewellyn

For more than 90 years Llewellyn has brought its readers knowledge in the fields of metaphysics and human potential. Learn about the newest books in spiritual guidance, natural healing, astrology, occult philosophy, and more. Enjoy book reviews, new age articles, a calender of events, plus current products and services. To get your free copy of *Llewellyn's New Worlds of Mind and Spirit*, send your name and address to:

Llewellyn's New Worlds of Mind and Spirit
P.O. Box 64383-735, St. Paul, MN 55164-0383, U.S.A.

LLEWELLYN'S VANGUARD SERIES

The Truth About

EGYPTIAN MAGICK

by Gerald & Betty Schueler

1995
Llewellyn Publications
St. Paul, MN 55164-0383, U.S.A.

FIRST EDITION, 1991
SECOND EDITION
First Printing, 1995

International Standard Book Number: 0-87542-735-9

LLEWELLYN PUBLICATIONS
A Division of Llewellyn Worldwide, Ltd.
P.O. Box 64383, St. Paul, MN 55164-0383

Other Books by Gerald and Betty Schueler:

An Advanced Guide to Enochian Magick
Egyptian Magick
Enochian Magick: A Practical Manual
Enochian Physics:
    The Structure of the Magickal Universe
The Enochian Tarot
Enochian Yoga
The Enochian Workbook

WHY WE SHOULD STUDY
EGYPTIAN MAGICK

Modern humanity is the sum total of its past. The great Swiss psychologist Carl Jung once wrote:

> The individual is the only reality . . . In these times of social upheaval and rapid change, it is desirable to know much more than we do about the individual human being, for so much depends upon his mental and moral qualities. But if we are able to see things in their right perspective, we need to understand the past of man as well as his present. That is why an understanding of myths and symbols is of essential importance. (*Man and His Symbols*)

Egyptian Magic—spelled with a "k" to differentiate it from stage magic or sleight of hand—is one of the first recorded human efforts to symbolically define the inner and outer cosmos—the microcosm and the macrocosm. Developed over a period of 6,000 years, it is the most powerful form of symbolism ever devised. It has survived countless attacks from foreign ideologies. It reaches below our conscious minds to tap into the collective unconsciousness of humankind. The symbols of ancient Egypt are still alive today, because they still exist in the hearts and minds of living people.

The most famous magician of this century, Aleister Crowley, once wrote:

> The Egyptian Theogony is the noblest, the most truly magical . . . I use it (with its Graeco-Phoenician child) for all work of supreme import. (*Magick Without Tears*)

His one-time secretary, Israel Regardie, wrote:

> It was in Egypt, so far as the western form of magic is concerned, that these cosmic forces received close attention and their qualities and attributes were observed and recorded. Thus arose the conventionalized pictographs of their gods which are profound in significance, while simple in the moving eloquence of their description. It is the Egyptian god-forms that are used in occidental magic, not those of Tibet or India. (*The Art and Meaning of Magic*)

It is truly amazing that the symbolic deities of the ancient Egyptians still hold power in today's world of computers and rocket ships. The gods and goddesses of Egypt were powerful thought-forms which were built up, and animated, by the collective thinking of the ancient Egyptians. The psychic forces these deities represent are still present today, lying deep within the collective unconsciousness of you and me. Just as our physical bodies are the evolutionary inheritance of our forefathers, so the symbolic deities of the ancient Egyptians are the archetypes of our subconscious mind. Before we can understand ourselves and our role in this world, we must first understand the roots from which we sprang.

A SHORT HISTORY OF WESTERN INTEREST IN ANCIENT EGYPT

Modern, western man first became enthralled with ancient Egypt after the infamous military expedition of Napoleon Bonaparte in 1798. Although the primary purpose of Napoleon's expedition was to conquer and colonize Egypt, Napoleon took some 500 civilian scientists, artists, and workmen along with his 36,000 troops. Their purpose was to study and record the natural history, geography, and monuments of Egypt. The results of this exhaustive research were published in the early 1800s in the *Description de l'Egypte*, one of the most magnificent collective works ever published. The books included engravings, maps, and essays which described in minute detail the wonders of this ancient civilization.

It was during the expedition of 1798 that an artillery officer named Boussard found a mysterious engraved stone, called a stele, among the ruins of Fort Saint Julian near the Rosetta mouth of the Nile. It is called the Rosetta Stone and now rests in the British Museum. It records that Ptolemy V Epiphanes, king of Egypt from B.C. 205 to B.C. 182, gave great gifts to the priesthood, provided money for temple maintenance, and did other charitable works. In return, the priesthood erected a statue of the king in every temple throughout Egypt. The message was written in three different ways: in hieroglyphics, in demotic (a written form of Egyptian), and in Greek characters. Some of France's best scholars went to work on this stele, including Jean Francois Champollion, and discovered that the Egyptian hieroglyphics included alphabetical letters that formed sounds just like any modern alphabet. Soon the code was broken, and translations of Egyptian hieroglyphics became a reality.

A little over a hundred years later, another incident took place which captured the fancy of the public as few other events in history have. In November 1922, an archaeologist named Howard Carter made what was probably the most famous archaeological discovery of the century—the tomb of the 18th Dynasty boy-king Tut-Ankh-Amen (Tutankhamen), "the living image of Amen." Originally named Tut-Ankh-Aten, this famous son of Amenhotep III picked up the pieces after the disastrous reign of his brother, the Heretic King, Akhenaten. He became king at nine or ten years of age and ruled for only about ten years. In all, he was a relatively minor king of Egypt. The enormous treasures left in his small tomb, however, made everyone speculate about what vast treasures must have accompanied the burials of the truly great kings.

The tomb of Tutankhamen lay in the Valley of the Kings, across the Nile from Luxor. On November 26, 1922, Carter, together with his assistant, A. R. Callender; his benefactor, Lord Carnarvon; and his daughter, Lady Evelyn Herbert, became the first living people to enter the tomb since it had been sealed shut by the ancient Egyptian priests. As Carter's eyes grew accustomed to the light, "details of the room within emerged slowly from the mist, strange animals, statues, and gold—everywhere the glint of gold." Then Lord Carnarvon asked, "Can you see anything?" Carter replied, "Yes, wonderful things." (*The Discovery of the Tomb of Tutankhamen* by Howard Carter and A. C. Mace.) Carter spent the next ten years excavating and cataloging the contents of the tomb.

The press had a field day with the discovery. Not only did the tomb reveal great wealth, it also appeared to have a curse protecting it. At almost the exact time Carter entered Tut's tomb, the lights in Cairo went out without explanation. Shortly afterward, Lord Carnarvon was bitten by an insect and died. The curse of Tut's tomb made headlines around the world. People who had never had any interest in archaeology began following the sensational stories that were deliberately written to pique their interest. Mummy movies were quickly made to help whip public interest into a feverish pitch. Tut became a household name.

In the years that followed, other world events eclipsed the interest in Egyptian archaeology. The next spurt of interest in Egypt occurred when Russia and Egypt joined forces in 1960 to build the Aswan High Dam. The purpose of the dam was to provide electricity for the people of Egypt. Unfortunately, a side effect of building the dam was the flooding of the plains that held many archaeological sites such as Abu Simbel. The whole world became galvanized in an effort to save these incomparable archaeological treasures. Through the efforts of an international rescue program, the most important monuments were moved to safety. Those that couldn't be saved were preserved in photographs and drawings. As the waters of the dam's reservoir rose in 1970-71, the whole world mourned the loss of precious remnants of mankind's golden past.

Throughout the years that followed, Egypt was to remain constantly in the news for one reason or another. Public interest in Egypt's past was constantly rekindled through books, movies, plays, and new archaeological discoveries and exhibitions. The most popular exhibit in recent years was the fabulous King Tut Exhibit. For the first time, hundreds of thousands of people around the globe got to personally view the incredible artifacts that were found in Tut's tomb, bringing to one and all a lasting memory of the glory of ancient Egypt.

While general public interest in ancient Egypt has only developed over the last couple of centuries, there has always been an occult interest in the teachings of the ancient Egyptians. Long before Champollion broke the code on the Rosetta Stone, various occultists claimed to understand the pictographs carved on the tombs and temples of Egypt. This understanding gave them knowledge of the universe which was hidden to the uninitiated. Whether the claims were false or true, there is little doubt that many prominent occultists have had a greater understanding of the physical and spiritual world than their more traditional counterparts. In fact, modern scientists have only recently come to accept that there is more to the world than the obvious. As a result, a new interest has developed in the teachings of the ancient Egyptians, for these people were able to develop a level of civilization which mankind has yet to surpass.

A BRIEF HISTORY OF EGYPTIAN CIVILIZATION

Our first recorded evidence of man inhabiting the land which was later to become the nation of Egypt occurred about 2 million years ago. It wasn't until 7000 B.C., however, that man settled into agricultural villages along the Nile River and began raising stock. Some 4000 years would pass before man would form towns and develop crafts, architecture, and writing. It is unclear whether these people developed these skills independently or if they were imported from other civilizations. Regardless, the Egyptians of the New Kingdom (1551-712 B.C.) were able to refine these skills until they reached a level which would not be matched again for thousands of years. It was during this period that Egyptian civilization reached its peak. Close relations with western Asia infused Egyptian civilization with new philosophical thought, art, and wealth. One of the most notable changes in philosophy was the short-lived worship of a single deity, Aten, the solar disk, which was the first recorded incidence of monotheism.

Over the next thousand years, Egypt continued to prosper even though it was often ruled by foreigners. In 332 B.C., Egypt fell under the control of the Greeks. The Greeks, like the Egyptians, were very tolerant of other people, and Egypt continued to prosper with its civilization intact. In 30 A.D.,

Rome took over the rule of Egypt. It was shortly after this that Christianity was introduced in Egypt and spread rapidly. Rome controlled Egypt for almost 400 years, until 395 A.D., when Egypt fell under Byzantine rule and became a Christian state. Then, in 640, Egypt came under the rule of the Caliphates and became an Islamic state. Egypt continued to be ruled by one foreign group after another until 1922, when it became an autonomous Islamic state.

AN INTRODUCTION TO MAGICK

Magick is the deliberate use of the will to bring about a desired change in one's self or in one's environment. The bell, candle, sword, dagger, incense, cloak, rod, and other instruments used in the practice of magick are important devices which, by their appropriate symbolism, aid in focusing the mind on the desired result. Gods and goddesses are the personifications of the creative, sustaining, and destructive forces of the universe. The magician must evoke these deities in order to consciously control them and use them.

Magick can take many forms. The most generic of these forms are: Black Magick, White Magick, High Magick, and Low Magick. Black Magick is any magical operation conducted to bring about injury to others, or it can be an abnormal extension or preservation of the human ego. (It does not include injury brought about as an unavoidable by-product of protection and self-defense.) White Magick is any magical operation conducted for the common welfare of humanity and/or nature. It should be noted that personal and practical benefits from magical operations, other than those resulting in injury to others, are more generally White rather than Black; the improvement of the singular is significant to the improvement of the plural. High Magick is generally considered to be aimed primarily at the growth, evolution, and spiritual advancement of the practitioner. Low Magick has more immediate and practical benefits, such as health, protection, gain, etc. The distinction between High and Low should not be confused with the issue of White vs. Black in magical matters.

AN INTRODUCTION TO
EGYPTIAN MAGICK

Egyptian Magick is probably the cornerstone of all major modern religion, occultism, and Magick. For the ancient Egyptians, Magick was not only a religion, but also truly a way of life. One would be hard pressed to separate Egyptian religion from Egyptian Magick. The Egyptians blended the two together so as to be indistinguishable. Unfortunately, little of the actual religious Magick practiced by the ancient Egyptians is known to us today. This led many early Egyptologists to believe that the ancient Egyptians were little more than semi-ignorant savages whose primitive brains were simply not capable of philosophy and complex thought.

While it is easy to understand why the early Egyptologists had such a limited view of ancient Egyptian civilization, it is harder to accept for a modern Egyptologist. In the mid-1800s, Egyptologists had only a very small body of information upon which to base their conclusions. Modern Egyptologists are under no such handicap. An enormous wealth of information has been gleaned from the archaeological sites of Egypt. The easy access to personal computers has allowed scientists to study the artifacts of ancient Egypt in untold numbers of ways. In spite of this, modern Egyptologists have been hesitant to challenge the conclusions of the early Egyptologists. It has only been in the last decade that a subtle shift in thinking has occurred in the ranks of modern Egyptologists. This change in thought should help pave the way for new knowledge to be acquired from the world of the ancient Egyptians.

While scientists have been slow to credit the early Egyptians with sophisticated thought, occultists have always known better. However, they were unable to substantiate their position because they were, limited to traditional, Christian-biased translations of the ancient Egyptian texts.

It has been a great loss to modern man that the early Egyptologists let their personal religious beliefs color their translations of Egyptian hieroglyphics and hieratic writings. One such Egyptologist was Sir E. A. Wallis Budge, the late Keeper of the Egyptian and Syrian Antiquities in the British Museum, and the author of *Egyptian Language* (first published in 1910). This book is the standard source for virtually all books on early Egyptian writings. Unfortunately, Budge was convinced that the early Egyptian texts were mindless spells and incantations created by a primitive people. He steadfastly refused to be daunted by the facts, and thus he subconsciously distorted the meaning and intent of many of the texts he translated.

New translations, such as those found in *Egyptian Magick* (Llewellyn Publications, 1994), indicate that the ancient Egyptians were a highly intelligent people who recorded for posterity a complex philosophy that included the abstract principles of creationism, reincarnation, resurrection, divine justice (karma), monotheism, polytheism, and after-death judgement.

Because there was heavy commerce among the peoples of the Middle East, it is impossible to know exactly which of them originally developed these doctrines. Ancient Egypt was the "melting pot" of the ancient world. Its people were not only amicable to new people and new ideas, but they embraced them with a passion. As a result, these doctrines became an integral part of their philosophical system, and it is from the ancient Egyptians, that we have our first written records of these doctrines.

While the original tenets recorded by the ancient Egyptians have long since been altered by modem philosophical and religious groups, it is important that we understand the composition of our religious and philosophical foundations. We can use that knowledge to strengthen and improve our current religious and philosophical convictions. It is imperative, therefore, that the texts used to express these concepts be explained and translated with as little prejudice as possible.

THE FORMS OF ANCIENT EGYPTIAN MAGICK

The ancient Egyptians taught and practiced two broad forms of Magick—Low Magick and High Magick. Egyptian Low and High Magick included two primary types: The first, *ua*, describes the effects of a directed will upon the physical world. The second, *hekau*, involves extrasensory perception and its derivatives, such as clairvoyance and clairaudience. The word *ua* can be translated as "magical," and is personified by a "Goddess of Magick." One use of this term is when Ra, the Sun, is said to travel over his magical pathway, the apparent orbit the sun makes around the Earth. The word hekau can be translated as "*ka*-senses" or simply "subtle senses." It refers to the subtle senses of the *ka*-body. The *ka* is the body of emotions, the "astral body" of occultism. Hekau is usually translated as "magical power," but it is not the same kind of power as *ua*.

Egyptian Low Magick consisted of divination, love potions, healing spells, and the like. Egyptian High Magick concerned the development and cultivation of the spiritual nature of humanity. High Magick was practiced by the rich and learned. It was used as a path of spiritual development. The ultimate goal, as with all true forms of Magick, was to complete what is sometimes called the Great Work—uniting the microcosmic self with the macrocosmic Godhead. The Great Work is not only a philosophical concept, but it is also a religion in the true sense of the word. Both forms of Magick make use of specialized rituals, the best of which are included in *The Book of the Dead*. These rituals are as effective today as they were centuries ago. Many of them have been adapted and/or enhanced by the western Magick groups currently in existence.

THE ELEMENTS OF EGYPTIAN MAGICK

Egyptian Magick had three elements: the pantheon of gods, the places (regions) of the Magical Universe, and the components of the human body.

The Gods

The Egyptians believed in many gods and goddesses arranged in a variety of hierarchical orders. The best known hierarchy was the Company of the Gods (sometimes divided into a greater and lesser Company) ruled by Ra (Re), or a form of Ra, such as Ra-Hor-Khuit or Amen-Ra. The Egyptian word for god, or divinity, was *neter*. This word and its plural were used by the Egyptians in the same way as *El* and *Elohim* were used by the Hebrews. A working knowledge of the gods was essential in any magical operation. According to the texts, all the various gods and goddesses could be encountered in the Magical Universe by a qualified magician.

The Places or Regions of the Magical Universe

The ancient Egyptians called the Magical Universe the *Neter-Khert*. Neter-Khert is a general term for the subtle planes and subplanes which surround this planet. They are invisible to our physical senses, but they are nonetheless real. They are the etheric, astral, mental, and spiritual planes of modern occultism and Magick. The term also refers to the location said to be visited by the dead. According to the ancient Egyptians, life in these subtle regions was as varied and personal as life on Earth. The question, "What happens after death?" can best be answered in the same way as the question, "What happens after birth?" In other words, what happens in the Neter-Khert is dependent upon many interrelated circumstances, and contingencies are plentiful. Although the Egyptians did not have the word karma, they clearly understood the concept. It is expressed in their word *maat*, which means "justice." One of the regions in the Magical Universe is called the Hall of Maati, which is said to be entered by every person at death. It is governed by the goddess Maat in her dual aspect as the dispenser of both rewards and punishments. Everyone who enters this region must have his heart weighed on the balance against the feather of Maat. Where one goes from here depends upon the outcome of this judgment. Egyptian magicians, preferring not to wait until after they died, entered this region by conducting the Ritual of the Balance as well as the Ritual of the Hall of Maati.

Table of the Cosmic Planes

Egyptian	Occult
—	Spiritual
Abyss	Abyss
Sekhet-Hetepet	Mental
Tuat	Astral
Amentet	Etheric

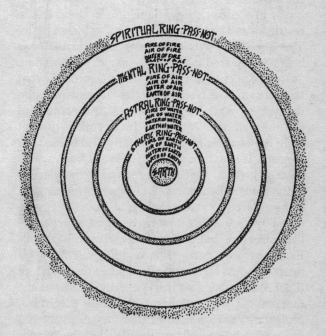

The Lower Five Cosmic Planes

Horus   Set   Isis

Anubis   Osiris   Nephthys

The Table of the Cosmic Planes compares the five Cosmic Planes of manifestation. The plane above the Abyss, for the Egyptian model, was a closely guarded secret, although regions such as Anrutef, Sekhem, and Annu (spiritual counterparts of physical cities with the same name) were said to be located there. Virtually all branches of Western Magick and occultism agree that the highest spiritual planes are separated from the lower manifested planes by a chaotic and impassable region called the Great Outer Abyss, or simply "the Abyss."

The Components of the Human Body

The ancient Egyptians believed that a person consists of much more than a physical body. The Egyptians divided the human constitution into a graduated series of parts. First was the physical body, or *khat*. Overshadowing or enveloping this body was a series of subtle bodies, each more ethereal than the last. The first of these, and the most dense of the subtle bodies, was the shadow, or *khaibit*. Next was the *ka*, the body of emotions. This was followed by the heart, *ab* (or *hati-ab*, which can be translated "outer heart"). The next was the soul, or *ba*, which was linked to the *ka* through the *ab*. The *ba* rested in the spirit-body, or *sah* (sometimes *sahu*), which was presided over by the spirit, or *khu* (quite often the word *khu* was used to denote the subtle body in general, rather than a specific component). These and other designations for human components were all governed by the highest, the *khabs*, the divine component which means "a star."

Table of Major Human Components/Bodies

Egyptian	Vedanta	Occult
khabs	atma	divine
khu	buddhi	spiritual
ba	manas	higher mind
ab		lower mind
ka	kama	desire
khaibit	prana	etheric
khat	rupa	physical

THE SACRED TEXTS OF EGYPTIAN MAGICK

The three elements of Egyptian Magick were defined in a series of sacred texts which were written on temples, tombs, objects, and papyrus (an ancient form of paper made from the papyrus plant). The most famous of these texts is the *Pert em Hru*. The texts came in two forms: the Pyramid Texts, which were written on the inside of pyramids, and the Coffin Texts, which were found in tombs. Other important texts included the *Book of What is in the Tuat*, which was written during the 18th and 19th dynasties; the *Book of the Day* and the *Book of the Night*, which were inscribed on the ceiling of the tomb of Seti I; and additional Pyramid Texts not included in the *Pert em Hru*.

The *Pert em Hru* is the name that the ancient Egyptians gave to a series of magical texts known to us today as *The Book of the Dead*. Many Egyptologists consider these texts to be religious prayers and rituals whose only purpose was to expedite the soul of the dead in its danger-fraught journey through the Neter-Khert (netherworld) to eternal life. In fact, as late as 1978, Timothy Kendall of the Museum of Fine Arts, Boston, wrote:

> ... the so-called Book of the Dead, the illustrated papyrus scroll so often found wrapped up with Egyptian mummies, contained a number of magical spells whose very purpose was the warding off of these and other horrors to ensure that the deceased would suffer neither want nor harm on his arduous, fateful trek on "the ways of the west."

While there can be little doubt that *The Book of the Dead* was used by the ancient Egyptians as a guide for the soul of the newly deceased, it had another purpose which was more pragmatic and functional. The *Pert em Hru* is a collection of sacred texts in the form of rituals and spells used by the magicians of ancient Egypt. Many address the various states and stages of the invisible worlds known as the Magical Universe or Neter-Khert. They provide advice and give guidance to the magician during the ascent into the subtle planes above the physical world of matter, as well as during the return back to the physical body. They consist of both rituals and spells and contain the bulk of known Egyptian magical tradition.

PURPOSE OF COMING INTO THE LIGHT

There were two main purposes of *The Book of the Dead*. One was related to High Magick and the other to Low Magick. The original purpose was to serve as rituals or teaching aids to magicians practicing High Magick. Many were scripts for initiation exercises. Some were recordings of experiences in the Magical Universe. Many offered ideas and visualizations in order to put the mind into a proper receptive state prior to a magical operation. The priesthood trained candidates in out-of-body experiences, which correspond to normal after-death experiences. The trained magician or Master could mentally go to any of these places in the Neter-Khert. The similarities between the "Coming Into light" of the *Pert em Hru* and the "Clear Light"of the *Bardo Thodol* (*Tibetan Book of the Dead*) are striking, and are in fact descriptions of the very same experiences.

LOW MAGICK USE OF THE *PERT EM HRU*

Low Magick use of the *Pert em Hru* involved reading appropriate chapters aloud over the mummified corpse of the deceased. This was done in order to direct, advise, and inspire the disembodied consciousness, which otherwise might succumb to strong forces of dissociation. Such forces were personified by the goddess Nephthys.

The Egyptians believed that consciousness survives bodily death and that the deceased, at least for a time, could hear the words read to him. Hearing was by means of a telepathic connection established by the reader-priest, who was called a *Kher-Heb*. The Kher-Heb priest, or Kher-Heb Master, was an Adept of the after-death state and was experienced in the states and stages of psychic existence that would be encountered by the deceased. After all, these are the very same states and stages of consciousness encountered in the Magical Universe, and these individuals were Adepts at astral traveling (traveling in the Body of Light). The Kher-Heb would mentally form a connection, or psychic link, between himself and the deceased. The Master would read aloud the words of the *Pert em Hru*. While reading, he would concentrate on projecting the thoughts behind the words to the disembodied consciousness of the deceased. Speaking the words out loud helped to focus the thoughts that the Kher-Heb Master wanted projected. The Master would unite with the deceased mentally by invocation and then speak the appropriate text. Throughout the process, the deceased shared in the experience. If the operation was successful, the deceased was transferred to the next stage, where a new text was read in turn.

HIGH MAGICK USE OF THE *PERT EM HRU*

In the introduction (rubric) to Chapter CXXXVII of the *Pert em Hru*, it is said that, "If this chapter is properly read for one, he will never lose consciousness." The rubric to Chapter XVIII says, "The recitation of this entire chapter can strengthen one. The rubric to Chapter CXLVIII states that, "This book should be read to every spirit, *khu*, so that his soul, *ba*, can come into light."

High Magick use of the *Pert em Hru* involved performing the rituals contained in that book. The reasons for doing so were various, but included learning about the Magical Universe as well as learning more about oneself. Certainly one of the primary goals was to be able to maintain a continuity of consciousness through the after-death state and thus remember one's past lives. The magical ability to exercise a degree of conscious control over one's life, and to enhance the prospects of the next life were also goals to be obtained. In most cases, magicians would practice both Low Magick and High Magick together.

THE USE OF ANCIENT EGYPTIAN HIEROGLYPICS

The word "hieroglyph" was first used around 300 B.C. by the Greeks. "Hiero" means "holy," and "glyph" means "writing." Egyptian tradition credits the god Thoth, the ibis-headed god of wisdom, as the creator of the Egyptian language.

Hieroglyphs were carved and painted on the walls of pyramids, temples, and tombs throughout ancient Egypt. However, only scribes and the higher classes could read and write. For the benefit of the working classes who could not read, texts were usually accompanied by pictures whose stylized rendering could be easily interpreted by everyone. Although early Egyptologists scoffed at the simplicity of these pictographs, modern man has devised his own set of similar symbols, the most famous of which are the handicapped sign, the women's room sign, and the men's room sign. Like the ancient hieroglyphics, these symbols represent universal ideas which people around the world can understand.

TECHNIQUES OF ANCIENT EGYPTIAN MAGICK

The ancient Egyptians employed many magical techniques to help in the practice of their religion. These included visualization, astral travel (traveling in the Body of Light), rituals, initiation, assumption of the god-form, appearing at the word, mummification, and sacred amulets and talismans.

Visualization

Visualization is one of the most important magical techniques a novice magician needs to learn. The imagination is an extremely powerful tool. Your imagination controls your whole viewpoint of your world. By employing your imagination, you can visualize people and places unknown to the physical world—the Magical Universe. Everyone is capable of visiting the Magical Universe. It requires only a vivid imagination and a belief that such a place exists. Reading through the various rituals included in such books as *Egyptian Magick* will help give you a feeling of the Magical Universe of the Egyptians. You might also want to consult some of the many picture books that are currently available on ancient

Egypt. Study the pictures until you can see the world through the eyes of an early Egyptian. Once you are able to do that, you will be able to correctly perform the rituals of Egyptian Magick.

Traveling in the Body of Light

The magician's Subtle Body, or Body of Light, is the chief tool used in some Low Magick operations and in almost all High Magick operations. Essentially, it is the living aura that pervades the physical body and extends slightly beyond it. It is shaped somewhat like an oval or egg (it is sometimes called the auric egg), and it contains colorful swirling forces of energy that, express thoughts and emotions. Although Magick uses the term "Body of Light" as though it were a single thing, the subtle body is actually composed of several layers of bodies. According to many occult traditions, every person has a physical body, an etheric body, an astral body, a mental body, a causal body, a spiritual body, and a divine body, making seven in all. These bodies vary from the most spiritual to the most material and are connected together by a psycho-magnetic link known as the silver cord. Consciousness is able to center itself in each of these bodies by means of this silver cord. During the day, consciousness is centered in the physical body. At night, during sleep, it is centered in one of the subtle bodies, usually the astral or mental. The magician learns to shirt consciousness to his or her subtle bodies, each of which has senses appropriate to its environment.

The general term for the environment of the Body of Light is the Magical Universe. As the Magical Universe is divided into many states and regions, so the Body of Light is divided into its subtle bodies. The magician travels about in the Magical Universe by shifting consciousness into a corresponding subtle body. While traveling about the Magical Universe, the physical body is quiet—as if asleep or in a coma.

Entering your Body of Light is another one of the fundamental magical techniques a beginning magician must learn. Begin by sitting in a comfortable position. Relax your physical body completely. Relax your body to the point of forgetting it, just like you do before going to sleep. Concentrate on where you want to go and then use your imagination to "see" yourself there. If you have mastered visualization, you should be able to freely travel about the Magical Universe of the Egyptians.

Rituals of Egyptian Magic

The *Pert em Hru* is a collection of individual rituals specially designed to aid the magician in out-of-the-body experiences. The rituals are a form of White Magick. According to Egyptian teachings, each person entering these spheres encounters experiences which are tailored to his or her own level of spiritual development. The chief function of Magick is to remind you, the magician, of your own inner spirituality and to help you maintain conscious control of yourself and your surroundings. The subtle environment, like dreams, is elastic and constantly changes to conform with the will of the disembodied consciousness.

Egyptian Magick is a means of control which must first be learned and practiced during life. Later, it is used in the after-death state to either ascend the planes or to return to life on Earth in the best possible manner, without the normal break in consciousness. The *Pert em Hru* contains prayers, such as "May I not be overcome by the disembodiment processes" and "May my season not come to an end." But there are also positive statements such as "I am the god Tem" and "I am fully conscious." In each case, these are reminders to the magician of certain key facts about the situation and advice for action to be taken. The statement "I am Tem," for example, reminds you that you are inherently divine and advises you to mystically unite with Tem by shifting your sense of identity. The shifting of identity is a major aspect of Egyptian Magick. When your body is hungry, you are apt to say, "I am hungry." When your body is in pain, you are apt to say, "I hurt." When your mind cannot retrieve stored data, you are apt to say, "I cannot remember." When you are aware of strong feelings of attraction and desire, you are apt to say, "I love" or "I am in love." Furthermore, you may consider yourself a musician, a friend, the driver of a car, a parent, and so forth. This ability to shift around your sense of identity is inherent in the human mind and is generally taken as a matter of course. The personality that you identify with during any one lifetime is the human ego. Although it seems real and substantial enough, it does not exist at all according to esoteric tradition. Its existence is completely dependent upon the focus of your sense of identity. A loss of this focus results in amnesia. A fracturing of it results in schizophrenia. Too strong a focus results in egomania, and so on.

The human ego is not a separate entity and will dissolve someday. Like a fist when the hand is opened, your sense of identity is a characteristic of the Reincarnating Ego or Oversoul. It survives the death of the body and even the most feared after-death state, the Abyss. The Egyptians were adept at the magical process of consciously shifting this sense of identity. It is the heart of their methodology for maintaining consciousness in the subtle regions and planes. It is the hallmark of Egyptian Magick.

When using the High Magick rituals presented in books such as *Egyptian Magick*, the magician will have to make various statements which, on the material level, may not be true. The statements appear to be egotistical, self-serving statements that attempt to deceive the gods. However, their purpose is to shift your identity from that of a human sinner to that of a noble Adept. They represent a psychological boost that is essential if this magical process is to be successful. Whether you are actually sinful is irrelevant. You must shift your sense of identity away from your human personality (the heart) toward your individuality (the prince, or mother). The reason for this is that the human personality will be annihilated in the Abyss (the region of dispersion). The individual will lapse into a state of unconsciousness and will wake in a new body with no memory of past lives. By magically transferring your sense of identity to that which is not affected by the Abyss, you can maintain full consciousness and deliberately enter a new life of your choice—with memory unimpaired. This Egyptian teaching is in full accord with esoteric tradition and bears striking parallels with other occult doctrines such as Tibetan Buddhism.

The *Pert em Hru* mentions at least six stages in the magical ascent toward full control and full consciousness. At each stage the initiate was given a corresponding title. The six titles in order of progressive advancement are:

Tep-ta	Master of the Earth
Tep-aau	Master of the Hands
Tep-het	Master of the Temple
Tepu-tu	Master of the Stone Mountain
Nes-khet	Master of Fire
Hra-tep	Master of the Universe

Egyptian Magick is a highly sophisticated doctrine which seeks to reveal the truth of humanity, the universe, and life itself. It consists of theoretical teachings and practical implementation of the laws of nature.

The basic magical doctrine of the ancient Egyptians is identical to that of mainstream western occultism: that the material world is a creative expression of the divine. Between the lofty heights of divinity and the grossness of matter lies an invisible universe graduated into a series of planes or states of existence. The lower portion of this Magical Universe was called *set*, which is usually interpreted as "the funeral mountain." As a mountain slowly ascends, and all upward paths tend to converge to a common point, so the entire Neter-Khert, or Magical Universe, ascends to a common divinity. An individual, the microcosm of the macrocosm, also contains within a graduated series of bodies, one for each cosmic plane of the Magical Universe. During the waking state, consciousness is focused in the lowest of these bodies, the physical. During sleep, and between death and rebirth, consciousness is focused in one of the subtle bodies, such as the *ka* or the *ba*. The thrust of Egyptian Magick is to enable you to leave your physical body in a subtle body (the term typically used for the subtle body was the *khu*) and explore firsthand the diverse regions of the Magical Universe.

The reasons for practicing such magical operations were twofold: to obtain general knowledge that could be used to explain what life was all about and to obtain specific knowledge that could be used to improve one's situation in the world. Two of the fundamental tenets of Egyptian Magick were first learned in this way: reincarnation and karma. The doctrine of reincarnation was taught in the story of Osiris and his sisters Isis (rebirth) and Nephthys (death).

Osiris was killed by his brother Set and then brought back to life by Isis, his sister/wife, using the power of the god Thoth. The consort of Thoth is the goddess Maat. Together, they represent the law of karma—Thoth is the faithful recorder of one's past words and deeds, and Maat is the dispenser of justice based on those records. Both Thoth and Maat are encountered in the Ritual of the Balance. The ritual is designed to bring you face to face with your karmic burden. The result will either be an ability to control karma to a degree, or failure to control it. In the latter case, you can actually become disoriented (eaten by the demon Amemit) to the point of either insanity or death. The rituals of Egyptian Magick are not to be trifled with by the unprepared (those unfortunates known as the "uninitiated"). You must be well acquainted with the philosophy behind each ritual before success can be assured.

The dividing line between Low Magick and High Magick is obscure. There is no clean break between the two. The rank of a Master of the Universe was obtained by successfully performing all of the High Magick rituals, but every magician had to start with Low Magick before advancing to High Magick. To become a Master of the Universe, you first must graduate through each of the magical grades as follows:

Master of the Earth: To obtain this rank, you must know such basic skills as reading and writing, history, and especially the fundamentals of Egyptian Magick.

Master of the Hands: To obtain this rank, you must obtain an appreciation for art and architecture. A Master of the Hands is an artist or mason of some kind.

Master of the Temple: To obtain this rank, you must obtain a working knowledge of the Egyptian religion and the general philosophy of the Egyptian people.

Master of the Stone Mountain: To obtain this rank, you must undergo the initiation of being placed alone in a stone sarcophagus within a pyramid for three days and three nights. You must be proficient at traveling in your Body of Light.

Master of Fire: To obtain this rank, you must have mastery of the vital force known as *prana*, and of the creative energy that circulates through the body known as *kundalini*.

Master of the Universe: To obtain this rank, you must have conscious control over the circumstances and events of your life and over your rebirth. You must become like the god Osiris.

The spells and rituals of Egyptian Magick are designed to assist any earnest magician in the progressive advancement to the grade of a Master of the Universe. Begin by mastering those in the section of Low Magick. For example, the ability to travel in the Body of Light is a prerequisite to successfully practicing High Magick. Similarly, the knowledge and use of talismans is a basic requirement.

More than 30 rituals and spells are included in *Egyptian Magick*. They are presented in the same form that they have been handed down to us today. Most are rather straightforward translations from the *Pert em Hru*, while others are collections of direct translations from various sources. All hieroglyphic texts of these rituals, together with translations sanctioned by modern Egyptology, can be found in the numerous works of Sir E. A. Wallis Budge. The rituals themselves are obviously unfinished, lacking proper openings and closings in most cases. However, they constitute the major textual portions of full working magical rituals. As such, they can easily be embellished by you, the modern magician, to serve your purposes. They also contain the core teachings (akin to the so-called *pith* instructions of Tibetan Buddhism) of Egyptian Magick. They constitute, even in their unfinished condition, what has sometimes been called the fountain source of western occultism.

Before conducting a ritual, it will be necessary for the novice magician to first learn the basics of conducting a ritual. These include drawing a magical circle, consecrating the circle, banishing unwanted forces, and invoking helpful forces. You will also have to learn the ritual you want to perform and then be able to conduct a banishing ritual after the ceremony is completed. This information can be found in many books on magic, including *An Advanced Guide to Enochian Magick* and *The Golden Dawn* (both available from Llewellyn).

In conducting a ritual, you will need to use materials which have magical correspondences to the desired result. Useful materials such as an appropriate magical instrument or device, incense, jewelry, and colors can all be used effectively. Such magical devices are aids to help the mind focus clearly on the desired result. Appropriate materials to use can be found in books on Magick such as Crowley's *Liber 777*. At the main stage of some ritual, you will be expected to enter your Body of Light and, using your magical imagination, visualize the appropriate deities and places as necessary. Whatever the case, remember to always use a banishing ritual afterwards, to sever all psycho-magnetic links with the magical beings or forces that you invoked.

If you are conducting a ritual which requires you to enter your Body of Light, you will have to memorize the words to say before-hand. Some rituals can be conducted in the physical body, and quite often these can be used as preparatory rituals conducted prior to actually entering your Body of Light.

Initiation

An initiation is a new beginning. When used in terms of Magick and occultism, initiation always implies a new experience, usually of a spiritual nature, which is difficult to put properly into words. In Magick, rituals are often used for initiations where the result of the ritual is a more profound understanding of oneself and one's world.

Quite often it implies directly seeing a region of the magical universe or a god or goddess of such a region. The ancient Egyptians used initiation rituals to produce spiritual trance-like mental states identical to the state called *samadhi* in yoga.

Assumption of the God-Form

An important part of many magical operations was a technique called the assumption of the god-form. The magician was to assume the form of a god or goddess and then act as if he or she were that deity. This "assuming the form" was not a physical act. The magician transferred his or her consciousness to his or her Body of Light and then caused that subtle body to assume the form of the god or goddess. The material of the subtle body is made of an elastic substance that reflects thought. As thought changes, so the subtle body changes. If you are a magician conducting a ritual and you are told to "assume the god-form of Tem," for example, you must adjust your subtle body so that it conforms in your magical imagination to the god Tem. If the god or goddess is usually shown holding an object, you must hold a similar object. If the god or goddess usually holds a certain pose or stance, you must try to simulate it. In addition to appearance, you must also temporarily assume the personality characteristics of the god. You must, in short, identify yourself with the god or goddess as much as possible. To do this, you need to know the characteristics of each deity before conducting the ritual. The modern magician would do well to consult *The Gods of the Egyptians*, in two volumes, by Wallis Budge, before trying to assume an Egyptian god-form.

For example, to assume the god-form of Horus the child (Harpocrates), you might place your index finger against your lower lip like Horus is often shown doing. If you want your god-form to be authoritative, you might hold a scepter, the symbol for power and authority. A god-form of Ra might hold an ankh, the symbol of life, and so on. If holding a physical object helps you to produce a god-form, then do so. If imagining such an object is just as easy for you, then use your imagination to construct a *thought-form* of the object. To perform these rituals successfully, you must be able to feel that you are the deity. Whatever it takes to do this is what you should use. There are no hard and fast rules.

The Power of Words

Words were considered powerful in a magical sense. To know the name of something gave one power over it. According to *The Ritual of Isis and Ra*, "the life of a person is invested in his name." This teaching became one of the hallmarks of western Magick, culminating in the idea of pronouncing "magick words" in order to effect a magical operation. The importance of names was also well known in India. The serious student should read *The Garland of Letters* by Sir John Woodroffe (Ganesh & Co., distributed by Vedanta Press), where the esoteric teachings of sound and natural names, shared by the ancient Egyptians, are clearly detailed.

Another important magical operation involving words was called *appearing at the word*. The Egyptian magicians taught that things could be made to "come forth at the word." A typical writing for a ritual would be:

> May these be given appearance at the word: bread, drink, oxen, fowl, clothing, and incense for breathing the sweet air of life.

In order to help feed a deceased or disembodied person, for example, an Egyptian magician or priest could say out loud the name of a thing, such as bread, while concentrating on an image of bread. This would actually make an astral counterpart of bread available for the deceased who was in an astral body. Such astral projections of articles were typical in the Middle and New Kingdoms. In earlier times, the "appearing at the word" was done physically. This magical technique is called "precipitation," where mental images were actually manifested physically by the magical will of the priest or magician.

Mummification

The god Osiris was slain by his brother, Set. His sister/wife, Isis, with the help of Thoth, the god of wisdom, was able to resurrect him in Amentet, the City in the West. In this way, Osiris became the god of the dead. The magical operation used by Isis and Thoth to affect this, was mummification. By using the same process of mummifying the body of a deceased person, the priesthood was symbolically associating that person with the god Osiris. Ani thus became the Osiris Ani. Tutankhamen became the Osiris Tutankhamen, and so on. As Osiris was translated to Amentet to live in the subtle planes as a King and Lord, so any individual could be resurrected by the same magical process. Such was the general religious interpretation of this operation. However, a more esoteric explanation was known by those who were initiated into the higher mysteries.

The god Osiris-Khenti-Amenti was the Egyptian equivalent of the eastern *nirmanakaya*. Osiris, the Initiator in Amentet, was a special title given to certain Adepts who desired to remain in the general atmosphere of the Earth in order to help mankind. The eastern nirmanakaya was also such an Adept. The idea was to retain all of the lower subtle bodies and thereby remain in the etheric and lower astral planes that envelop the Earth as its planetary aura. They could teach and otherwise communicate with mankind by telepathic contact. They remained in the vicinity of the Earth and projected good thoughts and uplifting ideas into the general atmosphere of the world. Thus they acted as a calming spiritual influence on mankind. The magical process of mummification helped such Adepts to establish and maintain their position in these spheres by providing them with a permanent link with the Earth. Although the main psycho-magnetic link, called the silver cord, severs at death, the individual link with each life-atom that forms the body is still intact. While cremation helps consciousness to break with the Earth, and return to its home in the spiritual realms more quickly, mummification allows consciousness to postpone that break.

Because the mummy survived long periods of time, after the fall of the Egyptian empire it was believed that pieces of a mummy could be used to effect powerful magical operations. By the law of correspondences, it was believed that a piece of mummy placed in an appropriate potion could give long life to anyone consuming it. Many tombs have been robbed, and mummies destroyed, in order to obtain pieces of mummies that could be used in such Low Magick operations.

Amulets and Talismans

Amulets and talismans were important magical devices used in Egyptian Magick. Amulets were used primarily for protection and were worn on the body. Talismans were used to invoke forces and were not worn on the body. Amulets were used by both the living and the dead, although the dead had to depend on someone else to supply them with the appropriate amulets needed to protect the body from decay. Three of the best known amulets and talismans were the Eye of Horus, the Amulet of Isis, and the Tet.

The Eye of Horus

Horus was the son of the god Osiris (who was the son of Ra, the Sun, and Nut, the sky) and Isis (who was the sister and wife of Osiris). The god Osiris ruled the cyclic process of birth and death, and the goddess Isis governed all forms of Magick and the processes of nature, both observed and occult. Horus thus typifies the resultant expression of those evolutionary and intelligent forces of nature (Isis) that combine with the unfolding cycle of reincarnation (Osiris). In this sense, the child Horus is a human being in infancy struggling to lift himself or herself from an innocent animal-like (karmaless) state into true humanity. The elder Horus is the prototype of the mature human being, one who is fully responsible for his or her actions. As with most of Egyptian Symbolism, an opposite interpretation also suggests itself. The elder Horus can represent the elderly person who acted with Eden-like innocence (old in the sense of the past), and the child Horus could be seen as the new individual who has attained self-consciousness and the karmic responsibility that goes with it (new in the sense of the present or future). The symbolism here can be quite correctly interpreted either way. However, it is in the third form of the god, the blind Horus, wherein the symbolism branches out into a complexity which is truly staggering in scope. Here, the key element is the god's eye, which the Egyptian's called *the Eye of Horus*.

What is the Eye of Horus? The truth is, it is many things. It had a multitude of meanings for the

Egyptians in the areas of cosmology, art, mathematics, Magick, medicine, and religion. According to myth, Set slew his brother, Osiris, shortly before Horus was born. Horus, after reaching maturity, avenged his father by fighting Set. During one of these lively encounters, Set stole the eye of his adversary and left him blinded. The ibis-headed god of wisdom, Thoth, retrieved the eye and returned it to Horus. The blind Horus thus refers to that period of the god's life when Sethian influences prevailed. For a time, the Eye of Horus was replaced with the Eye of Set. Horus however, eventually triumphed over his uncle and was given the title "avenger of his father." But what exactly was the Eye of Horus?

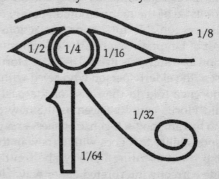

The Eye of Horus

In ancient Egypt, the idea of protection was expressed in the form of amulets shaped like the *utchat* (the right eye of Ra). These were very popular throughout the Egyptian empire and were made of all sorts of materials. The utchat amulet was believed to be beneficial for strength, vigor, protection, and good health. The reason for this can be found in the symbolism of the Eye of Set.

Set, the destroyer and opposer of Ra and Horus, is the very antithesis of Horus. He closely resembles the god Siva of the Hindu pantheon. Indeed, the Eye of Set is identical to the Eye of Siva. Siva's Eye was sometimes called the *deva (god) eye* or *the third eye*, the eye of spiritual vision said to be located on the forehead of the god. Occult tradition equates the Eye of Siva with the pineal gland of the physical body, which is said to correspond to a psychic power center called the *ajna chakra* located in the subtle body. The Eye of Set/Siva is therefore an occult eye which sees the spiritual realms that are invisible to physical eyes. The opening of this eye destroys the illusion of matter. It opposes physical manifestation (Ra) and ends the cycle of reincarnation (Osiris). Like the basilisk, whose glance turns an unprepared (uninitiated) man to stone, so the Eye of Set can be fatal to human consciousness and must therefore be fought against—that is, until one gains possession of the Eye of Horus. Only then can one be safely initiated by Set. The Eye of Horus clearly leads to one's perfection. According to Chapter VIII of the *Pert em Hru*, "My head is crowned by Thoth and is perfected by the Eye of Horus." Perfection is the goal of the highest initiations.

These hints show that the Eye of Horns is more than the Sun or Moon, a magnet, or a magical amulet, although it is certainly these things as well. In a magical sense, it is a special kind of conscious-

ness. The Eye of Ra is creative consciousness looking from spirit to matter. The Eye of Set is spiritual
consciousness looking from matter to spirit. The
Eye of Horus is a carefully balanced combination of
the Eyes of Set and Ra. Just as a human being
stands between spirit and matter, partaking of
both, so the Eye of Horus symbolizes the initiated
consciousness, rooted in the lowest matter but able
to gaze upward at the highest spirit. It thus symbolizes a view of nonduality.

The Amulet of Isis

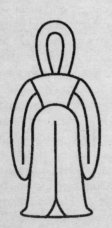

The Amulet of Isis

Chapter CLVI of the *Pert em
Hru* is very short. It contains
only five lines. Its purpose is
to magically charge a talisman called the *Amulet of Isis*.
This talisman can then be
used by a magician for protection when leaving the
physical body in trance or
during a magical operation.
The goddess Isis is the primary deity associated with
the forces of solidification and
attachment. She reigns in
Subplane of Solidification

which is in *Re-stau (the city at the pit of whirling*
brings together one's body components in prepara-
tion for rebirth, as well as maintaining a continuity
of consciousness for a magician who is traveling
out of his or her body. The chapter calls on the

blood of Isis, her magical power, and her spiritual power in order to preserve and protect the physical body after the mind and spirit have left it.

The Tet

The Tet

The *tet*, or *djed*, was an especially important symbol in Egyptian Magick. The tet is a pillar or column that symbolizes stability and firm support. The original symbol represented the spine of Osiris. It was formed from the hieroglyph for the spine, or backbone, which was mounted on a pillar or column. The Egyptians equated raising the tet with the resurrection of Osiris. They celebrated this event in a **Ritual of Raising the Tet** in Het-ptah-ka (Memphis), which was conducted by the king. The god Set was said to have *laid the tet on its side* while Osiris raised it up. In relation to the Body of Light traveling in the Magical Universe, the tet symbolizes the stability of consciousness. If on its side, then consciousness is faltering (such as a swoon or faint), whereas if raised, then consciousness is stable. The Egyptian magician would make a tet out of a metal or precious stone and then charge it like a talisman.

COMING INTO THE LIGHT

The Egyptian funerary texts are commonly called *The Book of the Dead*, but the title of Chapter 1 is translated *The Beginning of the Chapters of Coming Into Light*. The phrase *Egyptian Magick* is the Egyptian title for these texts. *The Book of the Dead* should really be called *Pert em Hru*, or simply *Coming Into Light*. The first word, *pert*, means "coming forth" or "appearing." The second word, *em*, can be almost any preposition. The third word, *hru*, usually means "day" but it can also mean "light" and "Sun." The phrase *Pert em Hru* can therefore mean "coming forth like (or with) the Sun (or day)" or "appearing with light (or the Sun)." Because light is a symbol for consciousness, this title refers to a process of Coming Into conscious awareness, especially when such a process is also highly creative. This process of creative consciousness was represented by the scarab god, Khepera, the god of creative manifestation and of dawning consciousness. Khepera was the rising Sun, and thus he was an aspect of Ra, the chief solar deity of the ancient Egyptians.

The book *Egyptian Magick* contains modern translations of the main hieroglyphic texts written by the ancient Egyptians. The translations were made in accordance with the rules first laid down by Champollion and recorded by Sir Wallis Budge in his *Egyptian Dictionary* and his *Egyptian Language*. The hieroglyphic texts by their very nature lend themselves to numerous possible translations. This book employs translations which assume that the writers were the originators of the fundamental principles and practices of Magick that have been passed down through the centuries. The influence of other religions on the early Egyptians has also been taken into consideration. The similarities between the doctrines of Egyptian Magick, Hinduism, and Buddhism cannot be ignored. The results of these assumptions is a collection of magical, religious rituals that sheds new light on the subject of Egyptian Magick.

Egyptian Magick reveals Egyptian Magick in a way that has never been done before. It challenges the established assumption that *The Book of the Dead* is only a collection of spells and incantations used to guide a newly deceased king, priest, or scribe through the heavens and hells of a primitive religion. It demonstrates that the texts now called *The Book of the Dead* were known as *Coming Into the Light* and were originally used by living magicians as powerful and highly effective rituals to be practiced as part of a complex form of Magick.

WHO SHOULD PRACTICE EGYPTIAN MAGICK?

Most individuals who practice Magick have certain traits in common. They are usually people who want to consciously control their lives— physically, mentally, and spiritually. They resist the idea that their lives are like leaves, blown helter-skelter by the winds of karma. They reject the idea that there is an anthropomorphic god in some far-off heaven who arbitrarily rules their lives, giving and taking to suit his whims. They are people who want to avoid unnecessary, unpleasant experiences and they want to enhance pleasurable experiences. Obtaining these goals is done through various forms of Magick.

Egyptian Magick is the first recorded magical system known. Its usefulness was refined over six thousand years of use. It obviously was a very effective form of Magick. Individuals wishing to understand and perhaps practice Egyptian Magick are advised to study *The Golden Dawn* by Israel Regardie (Llewellyn Publications) for details on Magick and magical ritual methods. Those wanting to practice Egyptian Magick in particular should also consult *Egyptian Magick*. The Egyptian rituals presented in this book are only outlines, fragments of the most important elements of the rituals. They are not complete rituals in themselves. For example, the student of Magick will not find the type of robe to wear, the incense to burn, the weapon or instrument to hold, and so on for each ritual. With few exceptions, only the visualizations and words to say are given. The student can find a wealth of information on corresponding incense, instruments and the like in *Liber 777* by Aleister Crowley. Each student is advised to use these rituals as guides and develop his or her own complete rituals by adding personalized details to them.

THE ROLE OF EGYPTIAN MAGIC TODAY

Egyptian Magick offers modern humanity an invaluable opportunity to understand the roots from which it sprang. Because of this, the artifacts of ancient Egypt are being studied in great detail in hopes that they will reveal new insight into our role in the universe. The art and texts of the ancient Egyptians is our primary source of information, and they are finding welcome audiences today. A few years ago, Egyptian art was considered crude and primitive. Today, it is recognized as a true and compelling art form. A few years ago, the Egyptian religion was considered primitive and shamanistic. Today, we recognize that the Egyptians had a very complex and sophisticated religion which served them well for more than 6,000 years. A few years ago, the texts of the ancient Egyptians were considered the rudimentary pictographs of a primitive people. Today, new translations of the ancient texts are revealing that the symbols of ancient Egypt were metaphors of the collective unconsciousness of humanity. Careful study has revealed that the ancient Egyptians created a complex, civilized society that has never been surpassed. We have much to learn from the wisdom of the ancient Egyptians if we are to survive the atomic age.

On the following pages you will find listed, with their current prices, some of the books now available on related subjects. Your book dealer stocks most of these and will stock new titles in the Llewellyn series as they become available. We urge your patronage.

TO GET A FREE CATALOG

To obtain our full catalog, you are invited to write (see address below) for our bi-monthly news magazine/catalog, *Llewellyn's New Worlds of Mind and Spirit*. A sample copy is free, and it will continue coming to you at no cost as long as you are an active mail customer. Or you may subscribe for just $10 in the United States and Canada ($20 overseas, first class mail). Many bookstores also have *New Worlds* available to their customers. Ask for it.

TO ORDER BOOKS AND TAPES

If your book store does not carry the titles described on the following pages, you may order them directly from Llewellyn by sending the full price in U.S. funds, plus postage and handling (see below).

Credit card orders: VISA, MasterCard, American Express are accepted. Call us toll-free within the United States and Canada at 1-800-THE-MOON.

Postage and Handling: Include $4 postage and handling for orders $15 and under; $5 for orders *over* $15. There are no postage and handling charges for orders over $100. Postage and handling rates are subject to change. We ship UPS whenever possible within the continental United States; delivery is guaranteed. Please provide your street address as UPS does not deliver to P.O. boxes. Orders shipped to Alaska, Hawaii, Canada, Mexico and Puerto Rico will be sent via first class mail. Allow 4-6 weeks for delivery. **International orders:** Airmail – add retail price of each book and $5 for each non-book item (audiotapes, etc.); Surface mail – add $1 per item.

Minnesota residents please add 7% sales tax.

Llewellyn Worldwide
P.O. Box 64383-735, St. Paul, MN 55164-0383, U.S.A.

For customer service, call (612) 291-1970.

Prices subject to change without notice.

EGYPTIAN MAGICK
Enter the Body of Light & Travel the Magickal Universe
by Gerald & Betty Schueler

(Formerly *Coming Into the Light*.) The ancient Egyptians taught a highly complex philosophy which rivals the magickal doctrine taught today. Clearly documented is a major element of the system, the Magickal Universe—the invisible realm that exists all around us but is hidden from our physical senses. Through rituals (which are provided in *Egyptian Magick*), the Egyptian magician would enter his Body of Light, or auric body, and shift his consciousness; he could then see and converse with the gods, goddesses and other beings who are found in these regions.

This book reveals Egyptian magick in a way that has never been done before. It provides modern translations of the famous magickal texts known as *The Book of the Dead*, and shows that they are not simply religious prayers or spells to be spoken over the body of a dead king. Rather, they are powerful and highly effective rituals to be performed by living magicians who seek to know the truth about themselves and their world.

1-56718-604-1, 432 pgs., 6 x 9, 24, softcover $19.95

THE GODDESS SEKHMET
Psychospiritual Exercises of the Fifth Way
by Robert Masters, Ph.D.
Here is the story of the ancient goddess Sekhmet, a form of the Great Mother related to the creative and destructive power of the Sun. Most importantly, this book presents Sekhmet as an archetypal force, guiding the reader into a positive direct experience of the Living Goddess, her teachings and life-transforming rituals.

As a result of Dr. Masters' direct encounter with Sekhmet in a series of telepathic trance states, he has received the teachings of the sacred books of Sekhmet that were lost, pillaged from the temples and destroyed by unbelievers. This is a book of the reconstructed scriptures and spiritual disciplines that will open its readers to the mysteries, supernatural powers, and mind-body-spirit transformations of Sekhmet. Half of The Goddess Sekhmet consists of Psychospiritual Exercises, which are techniques that can be practiced primarily as psychological exercises and as a way to improve the health and functioning of the brain and nervous system. By doing the exercises, the reader will increase the awareness of, and ability to use, more latent human potentials.

0-87542-485-6, 256 pgs., 6 x 9, photos, softcover $12.95

INVOCATION OF THE GODS
Ancient Egyptian Magic for Today
by Ellen Cannon Reed

Ancient Egypt—Tamera . . . a civilization that exists now only in its ruins—has fascinated people for centuries. Now this mysteriously enchanting subject is brought to life for modern readers in Invocation of the Gods. It demonstrates how the gods and goddesses of ancient Egypt can influence and benefit our spiritual and physical lives today through proper invocation and worship.

Ellen Cannon Reed presents a thought-provoking blend of ancient Egyptian deities with modern Wicca. Invocation of the Gods touches on the heart of the Craft: the Gods, and love and service to them. The book will also find a welcome place on the bookshelf of anyone who feels an affinity with the ancient Egyptians.

If you have read any of the books by Egyptologists and found them unsatisfying because they were about "other people's" religion, if you have looked at the ancient writings and longed to understand them better, if you have wanted to include the gods of Egypt and their magic in your own ritual practice, *Invocation of the Gods* will be of immense value to you.

0-87542-667-0, 240 pgs., 6 x 9, illus., softcover $12.95

THE BOOK OF GODDESSES & HEROINES
by Patricia Monaghan

The Book of Goddesses & Heroines is an historical land-
mark, a must for everyone interested in Goddesses and
Goddess worship. It is not an effort to trivialize the
beliefs of matriarchal cultures. It is not a collection of
Goddess descriptions penned by biased male historians
throughout the ages. It is the complete, non-biased
account of Goddesses of every cultural and geographic
area, including African, Egyptian, Japanese, Korean, Per-
sian, Australian, Pacific, Latin American, British, Irish,
Scottish, Welsh, Chinese, Greek, Icelandic, Italian,
Finnish, German, Scandinavian, Indian, Tibetan,
Mesopotamian, North American, Semitic and Slavic
Goddesses!

Unlike some of the male historians before her, Patricia
Monaghan eliminates as much bias as possible from her
Goddess stories. Envisioning herself as a woman who
might have revered each of these Goddesses, she has
done away with language that referred to the deities in
relation to their male counterparts, as well as with cul-
turally relative terms such as "married" or "fertility
cult." The beliefs of the cultures and the attributes of the
Goddesses have been left intact.

Plus, this book has a new, complete index. If you are more
concerned about finding a Goddess of war than you are a
Goddess of a given country, this index will lead you to the
right page. This is especially useful for anyone seeking to
do Goddess rituals. Your work will be twice as efficient
and effective with this detailed and easy-to-use book.

0-87542-573-9, 456 pgs., 6 x 9, photos, softcover $17.95

Prices subject to change without notice.

THE ANCIENT & SHINING ONES
World Myth, Magic & Religion
by D.J. Conway

The Ancient & Shining Ones is a handy, comprehensive reference guide to the myths and deities from ancient religions around the world. Now you can easily find the information you need to develop your own rituals and worship using the Gods/Goddesses with which you resonate most strongly. More than just a mythological dictionary, *The Ancient & Shining Ones* explains the magickal aspects of each deity and explores such practices as Witchcraft, Ceremonial Magick, Shamanism and the Qabala. It also discusses the importance of ritual and magick, and what makes magick work.

Most people are too vague in appealing for help from the Cosmic Beings—they either end up contacting the wrong energy source, or they are unable to make any contact at all, and their petitions go unanswered. In order to touch the power of the universe, we must re-educate ourselves about the Ancient Ones. The ancient pools of energy created and fed by centuries of belief and worship in the deities still exist. Today these energies can bring peace of mind, spiritual illumination and contentment. On a very earthy level, they can produce love, good health, money, protection, and success.

0-87542-170-9, 448 pgs., 7 x 10, 300 illus., softcover $17.95

THE ENOCHIAN WORKBOOK
Enochian Magickal System Presented in 43 EasyLessons
by Gerald J. and Betty Schueler

Enochian Magic is an extremely powerful and complex path to spiritual enlightenment. Here, at last, is the first book on the subject written specifically for the beginning student. Ideally suited for those who have tried other books on Enochia and found them to be too difficult, *The Enochian Workbook* presents the basic teachings of Enochian Magic in a clear, easy-to-use workbook.

The authors have employed the latest techniques in educational psychology to help students master the information in this book. The book is comprised of 11 sections, containing a total of 43 lessons, with test questions following each section so students can gauge their progress. You will learn how to conduct selected rituals, skry using a crystal, and use the Enochian Tarot as a focus for productive meditation. Also explore Enochian Chess, Enochian Physics (the laws and models behind how the magic works), and examine the dangers associated with Enochian Magic. Readers who complete the book will be ready to tackle the more complex concepts contained in the other books in the series.

One of the reasons why Enochian Magic is so hard to understand is that it has a special, complex vocabulary. To help beginning students, Enochian terms are explained in simple, everyday words, wherever possible.
0-87542-719-7, 360 pgs., 7 x 10, illus., softcover $16.95

THE GOLDEN DAWN
The Original Account of the Teachings, Rites & Ceremonies of the Hermetic Order
As revealed by Israel Regardie
Complete in one volume with further revision, expansion, and additional notes by Regardie, Cris Monnastre, and others. Expanded with an index of more than 100 pages!

Originally published in four bulky volumes of some 1,200 pages, this 6th Revised and Enlarged Edition has been entirely reset in modern, less space-consuming type, in half the pages (while retaining the original pagination in marginal notation for reference) for greater ease and use.

Corrections of typographical errors perpetuated in the original and subsequent editions have been made, with further revision and additional text and notes by noted scholars and by actual practitioners of the Golden Dawn system of Magick, with an Introduction by the only student ever accepted for personal training by Regardie.

Also included are Initiation Ceremonies, important rituals for consecration and invocation, methods of meditation and magical working based on the Enochian Tablets, studies in the Tarot, and the system of Qabalistic Correspondences that unite the World's religions and magical traditions into a comprehensive and practical whole.

This volume is designed as a study and practice curriculum suited to both group and private practice. Meditation upon, and following with the Active Imagination, the Initiation Ceremonies are fully experiential without need of participation in group or lodge. A very complete reference encyclopedia of Western Magick.

0–87542–663–8, 840 pgs., 6 x 9, illus., softcover $24.95

THE KEY OF IT ALL
BOOK TWO: THE WESTERN MYSTERIES
by David Allen Hulse

The Key of It All series extends the knowledge established on occult magick. Book Two catalogs and distills, in tables of secret symbolism, the true alphabet magick of every ancient Western magickal tradition. *The Key of It All* series establishes a new level of competence in all fields of magick.

Key 7: Greek—the number codes for Greek; the Gnostic cosmology; the Pythagorean philosophical metaphors for the number series.

Key 8: Coptic—the number values for Coptic, derived from the Greek; Coptic astrological symbolism; the Egyptian hieroglyphs and their influence in the numbering of Hebrew and Greek.

Key 9: Runes—the ancient runic alphabet codes for Germanic, Icelandic, Scandinavian, and English Rune systems; the modern German Armanen Runic cult; the Irish Ogham and Beth-Luis-Nion poetic alphabets.

Key 10: Latin—Roman Numerals as the first Latin code; the Lullian Latin Qabalah; the Germanic and Italian serial codes for Latin; the Renaissance cosmological model of three worlds.

Key 11: Enochian—the number codes for Enochian according to John Dee, S.L. MacGregor Mathers, and Aleister Crowley; the true pattern behind the Watchtower symbolism; the complete rectified Golden Dawn correspondences for the Enochian alphabet.

Key 12: Tarot—the pictorial key to the Hebrew alphabet; the divinatory system for the Tarot; the two major Qabalistic codes for the Tarot emanating from France and England.

Key 13: English—the serial order code for English; Aleister Crowley's attempt of an English Qabalah; the symbolism behind the shapes of the English alphabet letters.

0-87542-379-5, 592 pgs., 7 x 10, softcover $19.95

Prices subject to change without notice.

MAGICIAN'S COMPANION
A Practical and Encyclopedic Guide to Magical and Religious Symbolism
by Bill Whitcomb

The Magician's Companion is a "desk reference" overflowing with a wide range of occult and esoteric materials absolutely indispensable to anyone engaged in the magickal arts!

The magical knowledge of our ancestors comprises an intricate and elegant technology of the mind and imagination. This book attempts to make the ancient systems accessible, understandable and useful to modern magicians by categorizing and cross-referencing the major magical symbol-systems (i.e., world views on inner and outer levels). Students of religion, mysticism, mythology, symbolic art, literature, and even cryptography will find this work of value.

This comprehensive book discusses and compares over 35 magical models (e.g., the Trinities, the Taoist Psychic Centers, Enochian magic, the qabala, the Worlds of the Hopi Indians). Also included are discussions of the theory and practice of magic and ritual; sections on alchemy, magical alphabets, talismans, sigils, magical herbs and plants; suggested programs of study; an extensive glossary and bibliography; and much more.

0–87542–868–1, 522 pgs., 7 x 10, illus., softcover $19.95

THE COMPLETE BOOK OF AMULETS & TALISMANS
by Migene González-Wippler

The Pentagram, Star of David, Crucifix, rabbit's foot, painted pebble, or Hand of Fatima ... they all provide feelings of comfort and protection, attracting good while dispelling evil.

The joy of amulets and talismans is that they can be made and used by anyone. The forces used, and the forces invoked, are all natural forces.

Spanning the world through the diverse cultures of Sumeria, Babylonia, Greece, Italy, India, Western Europe and North America, González-Wippler proves that amulets and talismans are anything but mere superstition—they are part of each man's and woman's search for spiritual connection.

The Complete Book of Amulets and Talismans presents the entire history of these tools, their geography, and shows how anyone can create amulets and talismans to empower his or her life. Loaded with hundreds of photographs, this is the ultimate reference and how-to guide for their use.

0-87542-287-X, 304 pgs., 6 x 9, photos, softcover $12.95